RAINBOW magic

RAINBOW FAIRIES

FERN
THE GREEN FAIRY

By Daisy Meadows
Illustrated by Georgie Ripper

Silver Dolphin

S0-CAP-128

WITHDRAWN

Silver Dolphin

Silver Dolphin Books
An imprint of Printers Row Publishing Group
A division of Readerlink Distribution Services, LLC
9717 Pacific Heights Blvd, San Diego, CA 92121
www.silverdolphinbooks.com

Copyright © 2023 Rainbow Magic Limited
All rights reserved. No part of this publication may be reproduced,
distributed, or transmitted in any form or by any means, including
photocopying, recording, or other electronic or mechanical methods,
without the prior written permission of the publisher, except in the
case of brief quotations embodied in critical reviews and certain
other noncommercial uses permitted by copyright law.

Printers Row Publishing Group is a division of
Readerlink Distribution Services, LLC.
Silver Dolphin Books is a registered trademark of
Readerlink Distribution Services, LLC.

All notations of errors or omissions should be addressed to Silver
Dolphin Books, Editorial Department, at the above address. All other
correspondence (author inquiries, permissions) concerning the
content of this book should be addressed to:
Hachette Children's Group
Carmelite House
50 Victoria Embankment
London
EC4Y 0DZ

ISBN: 978-1-6672-0437-6
Manufactured, printed, and assembled in Pittston, PA, USA.
First printing, February 2023. KA/02/23
27 26 25 24 23   1 2 3 4 5

FERN
THE GREEN FAIRY

The
Fairyland
Palace

Maze

Forest

Orchard

Black
Pot

Meadow

Tower

Beach

Tide pools

Rainspell Island

She

Jack Frost's
Ice Castle

Tom Goodfellow's
House

Merry-go-round

Willow
Tree

Mrs. Merry's
Cottage

Stream

Field

Town

Mermaid
Cottage

Harbor

Dolphin Cottage

COLD WINDS BLOW AND THICK ICE FORM,
I CONJURE UP THIS FAIRY STORM.
TO SEVEN CORNERS OF THE HUMAN WORLD
THE RAINBOW FAIRIES WILL BE HURLED!

I CURSE EVERY PART OF FAIRYLAND,
WITH A FROSTY WAVE OF MY ICY HAND.
FOR NOW AND ALWAYS, FROM THIS DAY,
FAIRYLAND WILL BE COLD AND GRAY!

Ruby, Amber, and Sunny are out of danger.

Will Rachel and Kirsty free

FERN the GREEN FAIRY?

6

Table of Contents

THE SECRET GARDEN

"Oh!" Rachel Walker gasped in delight, as she gazed around her. "What a perfect place for a picnic!"

"It's a secret garden," Kirsty Tate said, her eyes shining.

They were standing in a large garden. It looked as if nobody else had been there for a long, long time.

9

Pink and white roses grew all around the tree trunks, filling the air with their sweet smell. White marble statues stood here and there, half hidden by green ivy. And right in the middle of the garden was a crumbling stone tower.

"There was a castle here once called Moonspinner Castle," Mr. Walker said, walking up behind them. He was reading from his guidebook. "But now all that's left is the tower."

Rachel and Kirsty stared up at the
ruined tower. The yellow stones glowed
warmly in the sunshine.
They were spotted with
soft, green moss. Near the
top of the tower was a
small, square window.

"It's just like Rapunzel's
tower," Kirsty said. "I
wonder if we can get
up to the top somehow?"

"Let's go see!" Rachel
said eagerly. "I want to
explore the whole garden.
Can we, Mom?"

"Go ahead." Mrs. Walker
smiled. "Your dad and I will get the food
ready." She opened the picnic basket.
"But don't be too long, girls."

11

Rachel and Kirsty rushed over to the door in the side of the tower. Kirsty tugged at the heavy iron handle. But the door was locked.

Rachel felt disappointed. "Oh, that's too bad," she said.

Kirsty sighed. "Yes, I was hoping Fern the Green Fairy might be here."

Rachel and Kirsty had a secret. During their vacation on Rainspell Island, they were helping to find the seven Rainbow Fairies. The fairies had been sent out of Fairyland by evil Jack Frost, and Fairyland had lost all its color without them. Fairyland would only be bright and beautiful when all seven fairies returned home again.

"Fern," Rachel called in a low voice. "Are you here?"

Here . . . Here . . . Here . . . Her words echoed off the stones. Rachel and Kirsty held their breath and waited. But they couldn't hear anything except leaves rustling in the breeze.

"It *feels* like there's magic close by."
Then she gasped and pointed. "Rachel,
look at the ivy!"

Rachel stared. Glossy green leaves grew
thickly on the wall, but in one place
the stones were bare, in the shape of a
perfect circle.

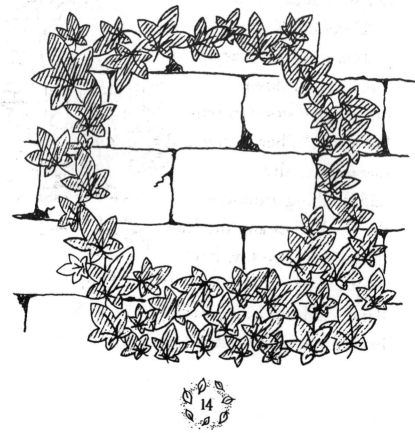

Rachel's heart began to beat faster. "It looks just like a fairy ring!" she said. She had heard that when plants grew in a circle, it was the work of fairy magic. She ran around the tower to take a closer look and almost tripped over one of her shoelaces.

"Careful!" Kirsty said, grabbing Rachel's arm.

Rachel sat down on a mossy stone to retie her shoe. "There's green *everywhere*," she said, looking around at the thick grass and the leafy trees. "Fern *must* be here."

"We'd better find her quickly then," Kirsty said with a shiver. "Or else Jack Frost's goblins will find her first!"

Jack Frost had sent his goblin servants
to Rainspell Island. He wanted them
to stop the fairies from getting home to
Fairyland. The goblins were so mean that
they made everything around them turn
cold and icy.

"Where should we start looking?"
Rachel asked, standing up again.

Kirsty looked at her friend and laughed.
"You've got green stuff all over you!"
she said.

Rachel twisted around to look.
The back of her jean skirt was green
and dusty. "It must be the moss," she
grumbled, brushing it off.

Dust flew up into the air. It sparkled
and glittered in the morning sun. As it
fell to the ground, tiny, green leaves
appeared and the smell of freshly cut
grass filled the air.

Rachel and Kirsty turned to each other.
"It's fairy dust!" they cried together.

WHERE IS FERN?

"Fern *is* here!" said Kirsty.

"Thank goodness I sat down on that fairy dust!" Rachel said.

They walked all around the tower, looking under bushes and inside sweet-smelling flowers. As they walked, they softly called Fern's name. But the Green Fairy was nowhere to be found.

"You don't think the goblins have already caught her, do you?" Rachel said. She was worried.

"I hope not," replied Kirsty. "I'm sure Fern *was* here, but now it seems like she's somewhere else."

"Yes, but where?" Rachel looked around the garden helplessly.

"Maybe there's magic around to help us," Kirsty said.

She looked down at the tiny leaves. Some of them fluttered across the garden. "I know, let's follow the fairy dust."

The bright green leaves floated over to a narrow path. The path led into a beautiful orchard. Rachel could see apples, pears, and plums growing on the trees.

"It's a magic trail!" Kirsty breathed.

"Quick, let's keep following the fairy dust," Rachel said.

Rachel and Kirsty set off down the path, which twisted and turned through the fruit trees.

Suddenly, the path led them into a large clearing. Kirsty's eyes opened wide when she saw what was in front of them. "It's a maze!" she cried.

The thick, green hedges loomed above them, their leaves rustling softly in the breeze.

Rachel nudged Kirsty. "Look," she pointed. "The fairy trail leads right into the maze!"

"We'll have to take that path," Kirsty said bravely.

The two girls followed the floating fairy leaves through the narrow maze entrance. Kirsty felt a little bit scared as the fairy dust led them one way, then another. What if the trail ran out and they got lost in the maze?

"Maybe there will be another clue in the middle of the maze," Rachel said hopefully.

"Or maybe Fern will be there!" Kirsty added.

They turned one more corner and, suddenly, the hedges parted to reveal the middle of the maze. An oak tree stood in the very center. The fairy dust led right to the bottom of the tree, then stopped.

"Fern must be here!" Rachel said excitedly.

Kirsty frowned. "Yes, but *where*?" she asked, looking around.

Tap! Tap! Tap!
The two girls jumped.
"What was that?" Rachel gasped.

There it was again. *Tap! Tap! Tap!*
Kirsty's eyes opened wide. "It's coming from over there." She pointed to the oak tree.
"I hope it isn't a trap set by the goblins," Rachel whispered.

Tap! Tap! Tap!

The noise was louder now. Slowly, Rachel and Kirsty walked around the tree. At first, they didn't see anything unusual.

Then Rachel pointed at the tree trunk. "What's a *window* doing in a *tree*?" she asked.

There was a small, hollow knot halfway up the trunk—and it was covered by a glass window!

Kirsty put out her hand and touched the window. It was very cold and wet. "It's not glass," she whispered. "It's *ice*!"

Both girls looked more closely.
Suddenly, something moved behind the
icy window. Kirsty could just barely see a
tiny girl dressed in glittering green.

"Rachel, we've found her!" she said
happily. "It's Fern, the Green Fairy!"

LOST IN THE MAZE

Fern waved to the girls through the sheet of ice. Her mouth opened and closed, but Rachel and Kirsty couldn't hear a word she was saying. The ice was too thick.

Rachel looked worried. "Fern must be freezing in there," she said. "We have to get her out."

"We could smash the ice with
a stick," said Kirsty. Then she
frowned. "But Fern might get hurt."

Rachel thought hard. "We could
melt the ice," she said.

"How?" Kirsty asked.

"Like this," Rachel replied.
She reached up
and pressed her hand
firmly against the
window of ice.
Kirsty did the
same. The ice
felt freezing
cold, but they
kept on pressing
against it with
their warm hands.

Soon, a few drops of water began to trickle down the window.

"It's melting!" Rachel said. "I think we can make a hole in it now." She gently poked the middle of the window with her finger, and the ice began to crack.

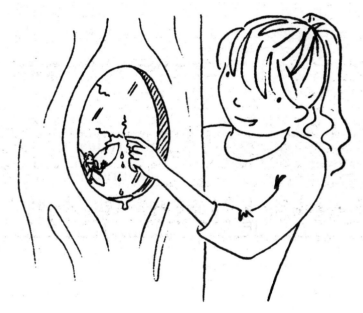

"Don't worry, Fern," said Kirsty. "You'll be out of there very soon!"

There was a sudden crack as the ice split open. A flash of sparkling fairy dust shot out, leaving behind the smell of cut grass. And then Fern the Green Fairy pushed her way out of the the tree trunk, her wings fluttering limply. She wore a bright green top and stretchy pants, with pretty leaf shapes around her waist and neck. She had  small, acorn-colored boots on her tiny feet, earrings, and a pendant that looked like a little green leaf. Her long, brown hair was tied in pigtails, and her thin, emerald wand was tipped with gold.

"Oh, I'm s-s-so c-c-cold!" the fairy gasped, shivering all over. She floated down to rest on Kirsty's shoulder.

"Let me warm you up a bit," said Rachel. She scooped the fairy up and held her in her cupped hands. Then she blew gently on her.

The warmth of Rachel's breath seemed to do the trick. Fern stopped shivering, and her wings straightened out. "Thank you," she said. "I feel much better now."

"I'm Rachel and this is Kirsty," Rachel explained. "We're here to take you to the pot at the end of the rainbow."

"Ruby, Amber, and Sunny are waiting for you," Kirsty added.

Fern's green eyes lit up. "They're safe?"

she exclaimed. "That's wonderful!" She flew off Rachel's hand in a burst of green fairy dust and twirled happily in the air. "But what about my other sisters?"

"Don't worry, we're going to find them, too," Kirsty told her. "But how did you get stuck behind that ice window?"

"When I landed on Rainspell Island, I got tangled up in the ivy on the tower," Fern explained. "I managed to untangle myself, but then Jack Frost's goblins started chasing me. So I flew into the maze and hid in the oak tree. It was raining, and when the goblins passed by, their evil magic turned the rainwater to ice. I was trapped."

Suddenly, Rachel shivered. "It's getting colder," she said. She glanced up at the sky. The sun had disappeared behind a cloud, and there was a chill in the air.

"The goblins might be close by!" Kirsty gasped, looking scared.

Fern nodded. "Yes, we should get out of this garden right away," she said calmly. "You know the way, don't you?"

Rachel and Kirsty looked at each other.

"I'm not sure," Kirsty said with a frown. "Do *you* know, Rachel?"

Rachel shook her head. "No," she replied. "But we can follow the fairy trail back to the beginning of the maze."

Kirsty looked around. "Where *is* the fairy trail?" she asked.

An icy breeze was blowing all around them now. The green fairy leaves were drifting away and disappearing.

"Oh no!" Kirsty cried. "What are we going to do now?"

Suddenly, they heard the sound of heavy footsteps coming through the maze toward them.

"I know that fairy is in here *somewhere*," grumbled a loud, gruff voice.

Fern, Rachel, and Kirsty looked at one another with wide eyes.

"Goblins!" whispered Rachel.

FAIRY FIREWORKS

Rachel, Kirsty, and Fern listened in horror as the goblins came closer. As usual, they were arguing with each other.

"Come on!" snorted one goblin. "We can't let her get away again."

"Stop bossing me around," grumbled the other one. "I'm going as fast as I can. OW!"

Just then, there was a loud *THUD!* It sounded like someone had fallen over.

"If your feet weren't so big, you wouldn't trip over them," jeered the first goblin.

"They're big enough to give you a good kick!" the other goblin snapped.

"Let's hide in the tree," Fern whispered to Rachel and Kirsty. "I'll make you

fairy-sized, so we can all fit under a leaf."

Quickly, she shot up into the air and sprinkled the girls with fairy dust. Rachel and Kirsty gasped as they felt themselves shrinking, down and down.

It was so exciting!

Fern took the girls' hands. "Let's go," she said, and the three of them fluttered up into the air and landed on a branch.

Fat brown acorns grew on the tree, as big as beach balls. Even the thinnest twigs looked like tree trunks to the tiny girls! Fern heaved up the edge of a leaf, which was as big as a tablecloth, and all three of them crept underneath.

A moment later, the goblins rushed into the clearing.

"Where can that fairy be?" grumbled one
of them. "I know she came this way!"

They began to search around the bottom
of the tree.

"How are we going to get back to the
pot?" Rachel whispered to Fern. "Kirsty
and I aren't very good at flying. The
goblins will catch us if we try!"
Fern laughed. "Don't worry! I think I
know someone who can help us!" She
pointed behind them.

Rachel and Kirsty turned to look.

A gray, furry face was peeking shyly around the tree trunk. It was a squirrel.

"Hello," Fern called softly.

The squirrel jumped and hid behind the trunk. Then he peeked out again, his dark eyes curious.

"Maybe he'd like an acorn?" Kirsty suggested.

There was a big, shiny acorn growing right next to her. She wrapped her arms around it, but she couldn't pull it off the twig. It was too big! Rachel and Fern came to help. All three of them tugged at the acorn until it came off the branch with a crack.

Fern held the acorn out to the squirrel. "Mmm, a yummy nut!" she said.

The squirrel ran lightly along the branch, his long, furry tail waving. He took the acorn and held it in his front paws.

"What's your name?" asked Fern kindly.

"I'm Fluffy," squeaked the squirrel, between nibbles.

"I'm Fern," said the fairy. "And these are my friends, Rachel and Kirsty. We need to get away from the goblins. Will you help us?"

Fluffy shivered. "I don't like goblins," he squeaked.

"We won't let them hurt you," Fern promised, stroking his head. "Can you give us a ride on your back? You can jump from hedge to hedge much better than we can! We have to get out of the maze."

"Yes, I'll help you," Fluffy agreed, finishing the last piece of his acorn.

Rachel, Kirsty, and Fern climbed onto the squirrel's back. Kirsty thought it was like sinking into a big, soft blanket.

"This is great," said Fern, snuggling down into the squirrel's fur. "Let's go, Fluffy!"

The squirrel turned and ran along the branch. Rachel, Kirsty, and Fern clung tightly to Fluffy's thick fur as he jumped out of the tree, right over the goblins' heads! He landed on the closest hedge. The goblins were so busy arguing, they didn't even notice.

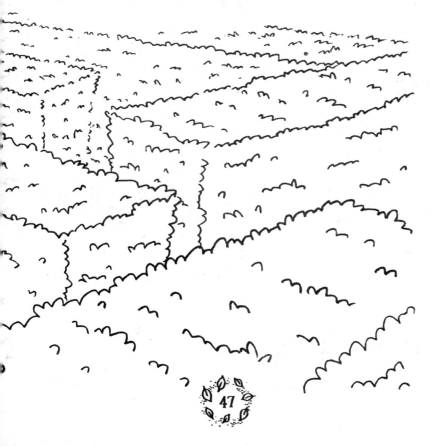

Fern leaned forward to whisper in the squirrel's ear. "Well done, Fluffy. Now, the next one!"

Rachel gulped when she saw how far away the next hedge was. "Maybe Fluffy needs some fairy magic to help him," she said.

"No, he doesn't," Fern replied, her green eyes twinkling. "He'll be fine!"

Fluffy leaped into midair. He sailed across the gap and landed safely on top of the next hedge. Rachel and Kirsty grinned at each other. This was so exciting! It was a bit bumpy, but Fluffy's fur was like a soft cushion. The squirrel was moving so fast, it wasn't long before they had left the goblins far behind.

"We made it!" Fern said at last, as Fluffy reached the edge of the maze. "Now, which way do we go, girls?"

Rachel and Kirsty looked at each other in dismay. "This isn't the way we came *in*," Rachel said. "I don't know the way back to the pot from here. Do you, Kirsty?"

Kirsty shook her head.

Fern looked worried. "But I have to get to the pot!" she said. "That's where my sisters are!"

"Oh!" Kirsty had an idea. "Rachel, what about looking in our magic bags for help?"

"Good idea," Rachel agreed.

Titania, the Fairy Queen, had given Rachel and Kirsty two special magic bags, for whenever they needed help rescuing the fairies. The girls took the bags with them everywhere, just in case.

Kirsty opened her backpack and looked inside. One of the magic bags was glowing with a silvery light. "I wonder what's inside?" she said, reaching in.

She pulled out a thin, green stick covered with sparkling gold stars.

"It looks like a *firework*," Rachel said. "That's not very helpful, is it?"

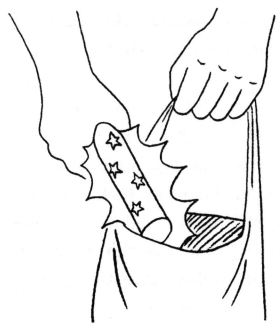

"It's a fairy firework!" said Fern excitedly. "I can use it to write a message in the sky, and my sisters will see it from the pot. Then they'll know we need help."

"But what about the goblins?" Rachel asked. "Won't they see it, too, and know where we are?"

Fern looked serious. "We have to take the risk," she said. Fern held the firework in one hand, her wings fluttering. She lit the top with her wand and quickly flew up into the sky.

Rachel and Kirsty held their breath. Fern and the sparkler shot upward, trailing bright green sparks behind them. Fern flew higher and higher into the sky, and used the sparkler to write a message in a shower of emerald stars. The stars spelled out the words:

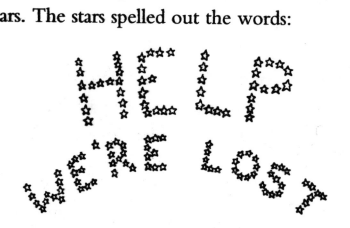

HELP
WE'RE LOST

They twinkled brightly in the darkening sky before fading away.

"We won't have to wait long," Fern said, landing beside Rachel and Kirsty on the ground. "Help will come very soon."

Rachel and Kirsty wondered what was going to happen. How could the fairies come to their rescue? They weren't supposed to leave the pot at the end of the rainbow, in case the goblins found them. Suddenly, the leaves behind Rachel, Kirsty, and Fern rustled.

HEDGEHOG HELP

Rachel and Kirsty looked at each other
in alarm. Fluffy seemed scared, too. The
goblins were on their trail again!

"They're coming toward us,"
Rachel whispered as the goblin voices
got louder.

"Don't worry," Fern said, smiling. She
didn't seem nervous. "My sisters will
send help quickly."

Just then, Rachel spotted a line of
golden sparkles twinkling toward them
through the fruit trees. "What's that?"
she whispered.

"Is it goblin magic?" Kirsty asked,
suspicious.

Fern shook her head. "They're fireflies!
My sisters must have sent them to show
us the way back to the pot."

Suddenly, there was another shout from
inside the maze. "Look, what are those
lights over there?"

"The goblins have spotted the fireflies!" Rachel gasped.

"Quickly, Fluffy!" Fern said as they all climbed onto the squirrel's back again. "Follow the fireflies!"

The golden specks were dancing away through the trees. Fluffy scampered after them just as the goblins dashed out of the maze.

"There's the fairy!" one of them shouted, pointing at Fern. "Stop that squirrel!"

"Come back!" the other roared as Fluffy ran off.

Rachel, Kirsty, and Fern clung
to Fluffy's fur as the
squirrel zigzagged
back and forth to
get away from
the goblins. Fluffy
scrambled up the
trunk of the nearest
tree. He was just
about to jump across
to the next tree, when
someone called to them from below.

"Hello!"

"Who's that?" Rachel asked.
She, Kirsty, and Fern peered
down at the ground.

A hedgehog was standing at
the foot of the apple tree.

"Hello!" he hollered again.

"The animals in the garden have heard that you're in trouble. We'd like to help."

"Oh, thank you," Fern called. Then she gasped as the two goblins appeared among the trees.

"Where'd that squirrel go?" one of them yelled.

Quickly, Fluffy leaped across to the next apple tree. The goblins roared with anger and dashed forward. At that moment, the hedgehog curled himself into a ball and rolled right into their path. Rachel thought he looked like a big, prickly soccer ball.

"OW!" both goblins howled. "My toes!"

Rachel and Kirsty couldn't help laughing as the goblins jumped around holding their feet. "Hooray for Hedgehog!" the girls shouted.

As Fluffy jumped from one fruit tree to the next, the firefly lights behind them began to go out.

"Hey! Who turned off the lights?"

wailed one of the goblins, still rubbing his foot. "Which way are we supposed to go?"

"How do I know?" snapped the other goblin. Their voices were getting fainter now as Fluffy hurried on.

"Thank you, fireflies!" called Fern, waving at the last few specks of light. "We need to find a way to the orchard wall from here. We can't be far from the pot now."

"If I were human-sized, I could probably figure out which way to go," Kirsty said. "But everything looks so big and unfamiliar!"

"But if we go back to our normal sizes, the goblins will surely spot us!" said Rachel. "I can help you," a small voice whispered.

A fawn was standing at the bottom of the tree. Her golden brown coat was short and silky, and she stared up at them with big, brown eyes.

"You mean you can show us the way?" Kirsty said.

"Yes, I can," the deer nodded, twitching her little tail.

"I can show you a shortcut."

She trotted off through the trees on her long legs. Fluffy followed her, leaping from branch to branch above the little deer's head.

Rachel was so excited she could hardly breathe. She was riding on a squirrel's back, being shown the way to the pot at the end of the rainbow by a fawn!

A few moments later, they reached the brick wall which ran around the outside of the orchard. Fluffy leaped up to the top of the wall, and Rachel and Kirsty looked eagerly ahead of them. On the other side of the wall was a meadow, and beyond that a patch of woods.

"Look!" Rachel shouted. "That's where the pot is!"

FLYING HIGH

"Thank you!" Kirsty and Rachel called to the baby deer. She blinked her long eyelashes at them and trotted away.

A blackbird with shiny, dark feathers was sitting on the wall nearby. He hopped over to them. "I'm here to take you to the pot at the end of the rainbow," he chirped.

"All aboard!"

Fluffy looked sad as Fern, Rachel, and Kirsty slid off his back and climbed onto the blackbird. It was a tight squeeze, and the feathers felt smooth and silky after Fluffy's thick fur.

"Good-bye, Fluffy!" called Rachel. She blew him a kiss. "And thank you!" She felt sad to leave their new friend behind. Then the blackbird soared into the air.

66

"Look for the big weeping willow tree," Rachel told the blackbird as he swooped over the meadow.

"I can't wait to see my sisters again," said Fern, sounding very excited.

The blackbird flew over the woods and landed in the clearing near the willow tree. Rachel, Kirsty, and Fern jumped down onto the grass, calling good-bye to the blackbird.

"Who's there?" croaked a stern voice. A plump, green frog hopped out from under the hanging branches of the tree.

"Bertram, it's me!" Fern called. Quickly, the fairy waved her wand, and Rachel and Kirsty shot up to their normal size again.

"Miss Fern!" Bertram said joyfully. "You're back!"

"We followed the fireflies," Fern said, giving the frog a hug. "Thank you for sending them."

"We saw the firework in the sky," Bertram explained, "so we knew you were in trouble. But you'll be safe here," he went on. "The pot is hidden under the tree. The goblins have no idea that it's here!"

Rachel and Kirsty hurried over and pulled aside the long branches. The pot at the end of the rainbow lay there on its side.

Suddenly, a fountain of red, orange, and yellow fairy dust whooshed out of the pot. Ruby, Amber, and Sunny flew out, looking very excited. A big queen bee buzzed out behind them.

"Fern!" Ruby called. "You're safe! It's so good to see you!"

Rachel and Kirsty beamed as they watched the fairies hug one another. The air around them fizzed and popped with red flowers, orange bubbles, yellow butterflies, and green leaves.

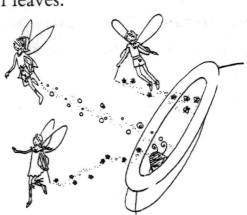

"Fern!" Ruby called. "You're safe! It's so good to see you!"

Rachel and Kirsty beamed as they watched the fairies hug one another. The air around them fizzed and popped with red flowers, orange bubbles, yellow butterflies, and green leaves.

"We really missed you," said Sunny.
The bee nudged her with a tiny feeler.
"Oh, sorry, Queenie," said Sunny. "This
is my sister, Fern."

Queenie buzzed, "Hello!"

"How did you get back so quickly?"
asked Amber. "We sent the fireflies only
a little while ago."

"Our forest friends helped
us," Fern said. She waved
as the blackbird flew off.
"Especially Fluffy the
squirrel." She sighed.
"It was sad to leave
him behind."

Ruby laughed. "Who's
that then?" she asked,
pointing at a tree on the
other side of the clearing.

Rachel and Kirsty looked, too. Fluffy was peeking at them from behind the tree trunk, looking very shy.

"Fluffy!" Fern flew over and hugged him. "What are you doing here?"

"I was worried about you," Fluffy explained shyly. "I wanted to make sure you got back to the pot safely."

"Would you like to stay with us too?" asked Amber. "You could live in the willow tree, couldn't you?"

"Yes, *please*," squeaked Fluffy. "I'm very lonely. I live in that oak tree inside the maze all by myself!"

Ruby turned to Rachel and Kirsty. "Thank you again," she said. "I don't know what we'd do without you!"

Fern fluttered lightly onto Rachel's shoulder. One of her wings brushed softly against Rachel's cheek, like a butterfly. "We'll see you again soon, won't we?"

"Yes, of course," Rachel promised.

"Only three more Rainbow Fairies left to find!" Kirsty added. She took Rachel's hand and they waved to the fairies, then ran out of the clearing. "We'd better get back to your mom and dad, Rachel. They'll be wondering where we are."

"Good idea," Rachel laughed. "If we don't hurry back, my dad will eat the whole picnic by himself!"

Now it's time for Kirsty and
Rachel to help . . .
SKY THE BLUE FAIRY.

Read on for a sneak peek . . .

A MAGIC MESSENGER

"The water's really warm!" Rachel Walker said, laughing. She was sitting on a rock, dipping her toes in one of Rainspell Island's deep blue tide pools. Her friend Kirsty Tate was looking for shells on the rocks nearby.

"Be careful not to slip, Kirsty!" called Mrs. Tate. She was sitting farther down the beach with Rachel's mom.

"OK, Mom!" Kirsty yelled back. She looked down at her bare feet, and a patch of green seaweed beneath them began to move. There was something blue and shiny tangled up in the seaweed. "Rachel! Come over here," she shouted.

Rachel hopped across the rocks. "What is it?" she asked.

Kirsty pointed to the seaweed. "There's something blue under there," she said. "I wonder if it could be . . ."

"Sky the Blue Fairy?" Rachel said eagerly.

A few days before, Rachel and Kirsty had discovered a magical secret. The wicked Jack Frost had banished the seven Rainbow Fairies from Fairyland with a magic spell. Now the fairies were hidden all over Rainspell Island. Until they were all found, there would be no color in Fairyland. Rachel and Kirsty had promised the Fairy King and Queen that they would help find the fairies.

The seaweed twitched.

Rachel felt her heart beat faster. "Maybe the fairy is all tangled up," she whispered. "Like Fern when she landed in the ivy on the tower."

Fern was the Green Rainbow Fairy.

RAINBOW magic

More Titles to Read

RAINBOW FAIRIES:
RUBY THE RED FAIRY

RAINBOW FAIRIES:
AMBER THE ORANGE FAIRY

RAINBOW FAIRIES:
SUNNY THE YELLOW FAIRY

RAINBOW FAIRIES:
SKY THE BLUE FAIRY

RAINBOW FAIRIES:
INKY THE INDIGO FAIRY

RAINBOW FAIRIES:
HEATHER THE VIOLET FAIRY

☆ ✲ ☆ ✲ ☆ ✲ ☆

BEHIND THE MAGIC

DAISY MEADOWS is a pseudonym for the four writers of the internationally best-selling *Rainbow Magic* series: Narinder Dhami, Sue Bentley, Linda Chapman, and Sue Mongredien. *Rainbow Magic* is the no.1 bestselling series for children ages 5 and up with over 40 million copies sold worldwide!

GEORGIE RIPPER was born in London and is a children's book illustrator known for her work on the *Rainbow Magic* series of fairy books. She won the Macmillan Prize for Picture Book Illustration in 2000 with *My Best Friend Bob* and *Little Brown Bushrat*, which she wrote and illustrated.

31901070300076